HOW TO USE THIS PROJECTOR

- Pick a clear space on a light-colored wall or ceiling three to five feet away.
- The biggest image can be seen when the projector is five feet from the wall or ceiling.
- Use Disk 1 to begin. Change disks as indicated in the story.
- Slide the picture disk into the slot in the top of the projector as shown.
- Turn the disk to the right as you read through the story. The numbers next to the text correspond to the numbers on the projected images. Use the focusing ring to focus the pictures.

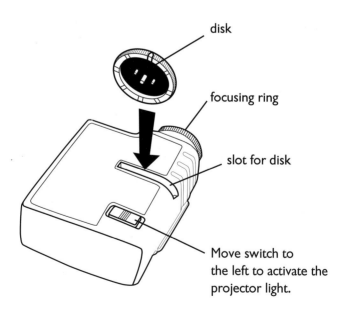

disk

focusing ring

slot for disk

Move switch to the left to activate the projector light.

PUPS
SAVE THE
PARADE

Disk 6

1

The pups were getting ready for the Adventure Bay Day Parade. In honor of the occasion, Marshall turned his water cannons into confetti shooters!

Zuma turned his vehicle into a cool pirate float. "*Arr*, shiver me timbers, dude!" he said with a giggle.

Meanwhile, Ryder was helping get Skye's helicopter ready so she could skywrite a big surprise!

Rubble was filling the bucket loader of his Digger with gray balloons that looked like rocks…and trying to keep them from floating away.

Over on Main Street, Katie drove up with a giant bathtub float decorated with pink balloons that looked like bath bubbles.

Cali and Chickaletta, each wearing a colorful shower cap, sat in the huge tub.

Alex helped Katie tie even more balloons to her float...

which made it *really* begin to float! Up, up, up into the air it went!

The tub—with Cali and Chickaletta still in it—drifted away until the giant straw on top of the lemonade stand snagged it.

A frantic Mayor Goodway called Ryder on his PupPad and asked him to help. Ryder immediately called the pups to action!

"We have to save Cali and Chickaletta AND get the tub down in time for the parade," he told them.

Marshall, Chase, and Ryder raced to the scene. "Ladder up!" called Marshall, and he rode his fire truck's rising ladder up to the float.

As Marshall reached for the pets, the float wobbled in the air, and a frightened Cali jumped right onto Marshall's face! "Cali, I can't see!" Marshall cried.

Marshall tumbled into the floating
bathtub. The force of his landing freed
the float from the giant straw and it
began to drift even farther away.

②

Marshall tried to steer the float,
but bumped into giant balloons
shaped like Rocky and Skye.
"Eww! A giant Rocky nose!"
said Marshall.

Marshall managed to steer the float away from the giant balloons, but then the tub bumped into the tower atop City Hall and Chickaletta fell out! Everyone watching below gasped.

"Net!" Chase cried, and the cannon in his Pup Pack fired a huge net over the area. Chickaletta landed in the net and bounced safely into Mayor Goodway's arms!

"Chickaletta!" the mayor cried with delight.

Meanwhile, Marshall and Cali were still inside the tub, stuck on the tower.

Suddenly, the wind blew, the tub tilted, and Marshall and Cali started to slide. Just in the nick of time, Marshall grabbed the tub's edge and Cali managed to hold on to Marshall's tail!

(3)   "We need Skye," said Ryder, and he called her on his PupPad.

   "Boy, am I glad to see you!" cried Marshall as Skye swooped over to him. With Cali still clinging to his tail, Marshall used his teeth to grab the bar from Skye's helicopter.

Skye safely piloted her copter down to the
ground. Cali rushed into Katie's arms for a hug
and a snuggle.

Marshall and Cali were safe, but the tub was still up in the sky floating away!

"Chase, you can shoot tennis balls from your cannon to pop some balloons!" said Ryder.

Chase began to shoot one tennis ball after another at the float. The balls hit the balloons and popped them, and ever so gently, the float sank back down to the ground.

The Adventure Bay Day Parade finally got under way. The team proudly drove down Main Street, beneath Skye's PAWsome skywriting and the giant balloons shaped like everyone's favorite pups— the PAW Patrol!

④

Studio Fun International
An imprint of Printers Row Publishing Group
A division of Readerlink Distribution Services, LLC
10350 Barnes Canyon Road, Suite 100, San Diego, CA 92121
www.studiofun.com

ISBN 978-0-7944-4135-7
Manufactured, printed, and assembled in Dongguan, China. SV/04/17
21 20 19 18 17 1 2 3 4 5

BATTERY INFORMATION

To remove or insert replaceable batteries, remove
the safety screw from battery compartment door.
Lift and remove door. Take out and safely dispose
of old batteries. Follow polarity diagram inside
battery compartment to insert three new batteries
of any of the following types: AG13 or equivalent.
Alkaline batteries are recommended. Put battery
compartment door back and secure safety screw.
Do not use excess force or an improper type
or size screwdriver.

GENERAL SAFETY AND CARE

- Non-rechargeable batteries are not to be
  recharged.
- Different types of batteries or new and used
  batteries are not to be mixed.
- Batteries are to be inserted with the correct
  polarity.
- Exhausted batteries are to be removed from
  the toy.
- The supply terminals are not to be short-circuited.
- Do not mix old and new batteries.

- Do not mix alkaline, standard (carbon-zinc), or
  rechargeable (nickel-cadmium) batteries.
- Prevent the book and unit from getting wet and
  avoid exposure to excessively hot or cold
  temperatures.
- Rechargeable batteries are only to be charged
  under adult supervision.
- Rechargeable batteries are to be removed from
  the toy before being charged.
- Remove batteries when not in use or discharged.

CAUTION

To ensure proper safety and operation, battery
replacement must always be done by an adult. Never
let a child use this product unless battery door is
secure. Batteries are small objects and could be
ingested. Keep all batteries away from small children
and immediately dispose of any used batteries safely.
Projector is not a viewer. Do not look into the lens
when light is on.

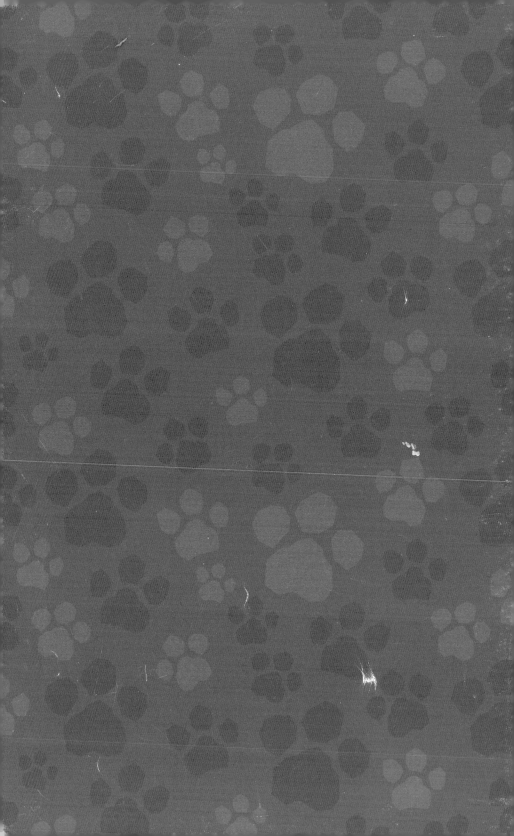